Mission Hunter –
The Battle For Eden

Denislav Yotsov

DEDICATION

I dedicate this futuristic allegory to my family, Zhivka, Beatric, and Theodor. I also don't want to forget my friend Ivanka Angelova for her support and editing of the book. I appreciate your support!

TABLE OF CONTENTS

STARSHIP "HUNTER"

Rock, what do you say? One hell of a battle! — Jeremy exclaimed over the radio.

You're right. There's an old Eden song that says this is our destiny to live as victors! The black giant laughed warmly.

It was one of those beautiful mornings when four of Eleal's ten moons floated just outside the portholes of the royal military satellite. The planet's pure atmosphere revealed the azure, blue-green waters of the mega-ocean below. Two landmasses, representing the continents of the eastern hemisphere, seemed to be drifting lazily in the vast sea. Majestic and immense, Eleal slowly and heavily rotated in its orbit, preparing to reveal its remaining six moons in a few hours. The door slammed shut, pulling the small group in the room away from the panoramic view. Captain Veren entered the small cabin where his new crew awaited him. His eyes swept over the faces of his subordinates, wondering how they would receive their new assignment. Just days before, they had been summoned to the Pentecost base, waiting for a secret mission yet to be disclosed. Veren took a breath. He seemed rushed. A faint smile touched his lips. The crew stirred, and tension filled the air.

Have we received the orders yet? A voice came from the far corner. A fair-haired young man, about twenty years old, stood up, his handsome face glowing with eager anticipation. The others' eyes also sparkled with impatience to hear the details of the mysterious mission.

Yes, Veren's answer was short and clear. His excitement began to show.

We must reach and liberate the population of the orbital station "Yoke," once called "Eden." It is now held by the Prince of the Air Dominion and the Dark Kings' Order he created. The captain took another breath, ending with a barely perceptible sigh of sadness. Centuries ago, "Eden" orbited the star cloud "Mercy," but it was later abducted and relocated to the constellation "Heart of Capricorn." The journey there covers about ten parsecs.* Three more ships from the Royal Fleet, finishing a mission in the Gavaon constellation, will join us. Veren paused briefly to catch his breath and continued:

This mission is extremely dangerous. We must not forget that the battle is for the Kingdom. So, don't be afraid that the Great King Himself sends us. The captain smiled and added:

More detailed information is available from the Hunter's onboard computer, the starship with which we will fulfill our Sovereign's will. Captain, I'm ready to fight, even die, fulfilling our King's will! The blond young man declared enthusiastically. Veren smiled at his heartfelt enthusiasm. That spark always touched his heart.

Steven, I'm sure not only you but every one of us here is ready to fight for the freedom of our Eden brethren and to fulfill His Majesty's Great Mandate. Steven nodded in agreement. About half an hour later, the Hunter's hangar opened, and the small crew boarded to explore. Entering through the main hatch, they found themselves in a modestly sized room with three corridors branching off. As they stared at the three directions, a small droid emerged from the left corridor and stopped five or six meters from the group. Ah, I almost forgot about you, TR-di! This is our onboard robot, who will show you around the starship. The captain gestured to Grace, standing nearby:

Follow me! I need to show you the command deck, where your station is. The only woman on the new crew smiled in response and quickly followed her commander. Her matte skin and the shape of her lips and cheekbones hinted at her mixed heritage. The two took the left corridor, leading to the command section. The other four followed the droid. After about fifty steps, they stopped under a large hexagonal hatch. We're in the heart of the starship. This is the gateway to the battle compartments, the robot announced in its metallic voice. From a small slot in TR-di's casing, three code cards appeared.

These are the cards you'll use to open the hatches to your skimmers. The three pilots took their respective cards. Steven immediately inserted his card into the code lock on the opposite wall. The hatch above them opened, and a small platform began descending. Professor, you may continue down the corridor to your lab, where you can use your intellect and talents to expand the Kingdom, — the machine continued in its steady metallic tone. The eldest member of the group smiled and looked in the indicated direction.

Not only with my mind but with my heart, I will serve our King! Two rows of pearly white teeth flashed across the professor's olive-toned face before Jadon moved forward down the corridor. The three pilots and the robot ascended the platform and vanished into the battle sections. The men followed slowly behind the friendly robot, which waddled proudly along the narrow corridor on its magnetic cushion. Reminds me of the old "Runner," one of the pilots broke the silence. His two-meter frame caused him some trouble moving as the giant often had to bow his head before the occasional crossbeam. Something else about his appearance set him apart, his chocolate skin. Looks like the old Brakma, right, Steven? Low and narrow!... — Rock, I guess it'll be hard to find a comfortable ship for you. "Hope there's enough room in the skimmer for your long legs," the blond colleague teased, directing the remark at him. The black giant squinted menacingly and showed his wildly white teeth.

A moment later, a deep, guttural laugh echoed behind those two thick rows of pearly whites. You always know how to put me in my place, friend. Maybe I should really stop complaining. Actually, I like this ship a lot. It's nice, even excellent... The last word was decorated with a quiet metallic chime as the giant energetically rubbed his forehead. If he had moved a bit faster, he might have bumped into one of his "favorite" crossbeams. "Are these our suits?" finally spoke the third man. And the weapons, too, added Rock. Here's the thermal sword and the nubilian shield. Without them, we're lost. We failed our last mission with the "Runner" precisely because we neglected our personal weapons. We thought we could fight just from the starship's deck, Jeremy sighed heavily. We barely escaped, Steven added sadly, his blond briton falling heavily over his painfully scarred forehead. The scar on my shoulder will always remind me of the foolishness we showed then. We forgot that our weapons symbolize our covenant with the Almighty Sovereign. Out of pride, we forgot that they are our only source of strength. The three men and the robot stood before three weapon niches where their gear was displayed behind thick glass. The fighters remained silent, gazing at the cases and recalling the events of their last mission. While the pilots examined their battle stations, Veren and Grace entered the command room. Impressive, Grace commented. I feel like I've stepped into a world of cutting-edge technology. And that feeling doesn't deceive you, the captain answered with undisguised pride.

The Hunter was built in the military factories of Golgotha. This ship is the perfect weapon. And I myself will be flying a machine like this for the first time. Veren motioned her to come closer to the panoramic window in front of them:

Actually, right now, we're on Hunter-1. It's the command section, but also a combat skimmer. Even when detached from the main body, the skimmer can remotely control all the ship's systems. Minutes later, the commander sat in his chair, opening the information block on the central computer. He began reading aloud:

We know that the station "Yoke" is located about 230 degrees southeast of the Equator, in the constellation "Heart of Capricorn," between the planets "Destruction" and "Void." The captain took a breath and continued:

On "Yoke," the Dark Kings' Order commands a powerful squadron, anti-air artillery, landing troops, and a high-tech radar system… A red inscription appeared on the monitor. Grace read it aloud with great satisfaction, emphasizing every word:

Stronger is He who dwells in our hearts than he who comes from the darkness! At that moment, Professor Jadon entered, his face radiant as always. With a slight movement, he adjusted his small glasses atop his Roman nose. Captain, I've inspected the laboratory, as well as the quarters, cargo bay, and hold. I'm satisfied with what I've seen. The hold contains the necessary types and sufficient quantities of ammunition, the professor reported succinctly. Not long after, the tour of the Hunter was complete, and the starship left the atmosphere that same day. Thirty-six hours after takeoff, the ship landed on one of the ten natural satellites orbiting Eleal, the home planet of the hunters.

On Galeya, we will synchronize the starship's guns. This is where the Kingdom's best firing workshops are located, Veren announced shortly before opening the main portal. After that, we have only this task left, then we'll head straight for the Heart of Capricorn. Tomorrow, the fifth round of the world speeder championship will be held on Galeya. Captain, Rock barely waited for his leader to finish.

Will we have any chance to catch a glimpse of the race? Not only will you "catch a glimpse," but I suggest we take seats in the stands of Galeyus Stadium and watch the entire race. Veren barely held back a smile. Jadon will compete as number six. I'm a big fan, so I'll be cheering loudly for him. A brief silence fell in the command room. All eyes turned to the professor, who responded with a slight smile and awkward scratch at the back of his neck. But this is the championship of champions, not amateurs... Wait, wait! "Is he the five-time Eleal champion?!" Steven exclaimed. Jadon van Doeren — the great Formula-Speed pilot! No wonder his face seemed so familiar, Rock almost shouted. His bass voice seemed to echo off the astonished faces of the rest of the crew. I can't believe I'm on the same ship with you, Mr. van Doeren! I'm your ultra... I mean — absolute fan, Rock bared his white teeth in a smile like no other supporter ever had. But you, Professor... or should I call you Mr. van Doeren? You raced more than twenty years ago. You're a legend, but how will you compete with today's generation of pilots? Jeremy asked, puzzled. The older man looked over the top of his glasses and replied with a thin smile:

The federation allowed me to participate one last time in this round of the Galeya race. It will be my farewell lap in FS (Formula Speed). When I was ending my career, the Fifth Intergalactic War broke out, and I never got to do my final lap. With that, the conversation ended. The elderly professor stood and followed his commander, waiting at the hall's exit. Despite his sixty years, Jadon had not lost the athleticism and agility of his body. During the three days of crew formation, the three young men constantly marveled at his youthful spirit and strength. Come on, guys, pick your jaws up off the floor and let's get moving. The woman from the Hunter pulled them out of their daze. After all, he's only one man, even if a five-time champion... Only a woman would say that! Rock muttered, annoyed by the last comment. After all, the great van Doeren is on board!...

THE "SPEED" FORMULA

Early the next morning, the "Galeus Stadium" began to fill up. Jeremy, Rock, and Steven entered with the fans who had spent the night waiting at the gates. Grace joined them an hour later, and Veren arrived just minutes before the race began.

"Jadon is ready. I've been in the pits with him until now. He said we shouldn't stop cheering. He'll need it," the captain nodded toward his crew.

"Did you see the other champions?" Rock hurried to ask. "Did you get their autographs?"

Veren pulled several postcards from his pocket and handed them to the three crew fans. Their faces lit up with immense satisfaction.

For an hour, Jadon had been preparing his speeder for the big... final race. And when the signal from the judges' tower called the racers to their positions, he started the engine of the machine beneath him. The roaring and then the powerful jet of air shook the "beast" below before it rose above the track's surface. A piercing roar sounded, and Jadon slowly moved toward the starting line.

Fifteen machines lined up at the starting line. Fifteen champions of Eleal stood side by side, ready to test their strength for the "Champions' Cup." The Professor examined his rivals carefully. Standing proudly atop their machines, the determination to win the title shone clearly in each of their eyes.

The starter's pistol cracked. The speeders roared, followed by the voices of tens of thousands of spectators in the stands. Like a wave, the sound spread from the start to the exit of the coliseum. Dust from the track mixed with the thunder of the powerful machines, and like a serpent, it trailed after them.

Jadon twisted the throttle to the limit and accelerated quickly. Two of his opponents were left behind immediately. Seconds later, another three saw Van Doeren's back.

The track ended, and the race moved beyond the stands. Hundreds of robot operators placed along the entire route would track the remainder of the competition. The massive monitors above the coliseum would broadcast the scene. The racers faced the valley of the Dark Shadow, had to cross the Forest of Confusion, and before returning to the track for the final straight, they would fly over the Bottomless Lake.

Soon, the convoy of speeders entered a narrow gorge between two sheer cliffs. Twilight shrouded the fast machines, and the surrounding walls echoed their roar with a ghostly echo.

This valley always made Jadon shiver. That feeling came over him again. But once more, he remembered his Redeemer. Peace returned, and a calm settled in his racing heart; that wonderful feeling of safety flooded his soul.

Suddenly, from behind, another racer appeared out of nowhere. There was a sharp scraping sound of armor, then the Professor's machine lurched uncontrollably beneath him. A moment later, Jadon would have been smashed into the cliff on the right. A chilling laugh mixed with the wild roar of the engine.

"I'll destroy you, champion!" the attacker screeched as he sped past.

The champion of the Kingdom of Mendor. This was the man whose father Jadon had defeated many times on the tracks long ago. "The apple doesn't fall far from the tree," a quick thought passed through the old man's mind.

With great effort, he regained control of his speeder and his anger. He passed inches from the wall, then hit the gas to make up lost ground. Several other racers flew past him, and soon the Professor was seriously behind. Still, he had one ace up his sleeve: he knew a path through the Forest of Confusion where he could regain the lead.

Soon, the sky above him began to clear until the blue opened fully. The elderly pilot barely enjoyed it. Dark green crowns of massive ancient cedars wove an arch overhead. Trunk after trunk formed an impenetrable labyrinth. But Jadon kept following the path he knew well.

After half an hour, the trees began to thin. The forest's end was somewhere ahead, and Van Doeren pushed the speed harder. Unexpectedly, from the left behind the trees, the champion of Mendor leapt out again. Without slowing, he crashed into the rear of the still-surviving racer from his first attack.

This time, Jadon couldn't react at all. Losing control of his machine's tail, he was literally thrown from it and felt his body wildly tumbling through the air. For a moment, he lost consciousness; when he opened his eyes again, he saw the ground from seven or eight meters high. He was hanging in the branches of one of the cedars. The ring on his breastplate had luckily gotten caught in many twigs. Now he hung helplessly between sky and earth. His speeder "obediently" stood about two meters below him and apparently wasn't seriously damaged, as its engine was still running. With several sharp moves, the Professor freed himself from his rescue loop and fell right onto the soft seat below.

Pushing the throttle to the limit, the five-time champion literally shot out of the forest. Endless waters quickly replaced the fading trees of the woods. The Bottomless Lake reflected the sun's rays and turned into a sea of fire.

The veteran removed his helmet and looked around. The wind mercilessly scattered his silver hair. A few of his rivals were just emerging from the forest. That meant he still had a chance to reach the top three. Although battered, his speeder could hold out until the finish.

Taking a deep breath of fresh air, Jadon skimmed low over the water's surface. Behind him, the water parted, forming a deep channel ending in billions of splashes. Soon, two of his opponents had the opportunity to deeply inhale that watery spray.

Half a kilometer ahead, the Professor spotted the leader. But in that moment, something or rather someone, flashed before his eyes, helplessly trying to stay afloat. The champion of Mendor was desperately fighting for his life. His speeder had sunk, and soon, likely, the owner would follow. Apparently, his machine had suffered more damage during the collisions than Jadon's.

Without hesitation, the veteran lowered his machine and jumped into the water. He was a good swimmer and soon dragged the drowning man to his speeder. The other racers zoomed past them without even slowing down. With great effort, Jadon managed to hoist the unconscious body of his "enemy" onto the seat. He looked at the bruised face, but it stirred no ill feelings inside him. Only regret was written in his gaze.

Half an hour later, Jadon Van Doeren entered the "Galeus Stadium." The last racer had finished just minutes before. Silence reigned in the coliseum. Tens of thousands of eyes followed him silently. Surely millions more watched the same way on their home screens. The veteran failed to win his final glory, but inside himself, he felt like a champion because he had managed to forgive his enemy, just as he once had been forgiven. And is there any greater victory than that? To overcome evil with good.

"JADON Van Doeren! Van Doeren, Van Doeren!..." erupted from somewhere a familiar bass voice. "Van Doeren!" The crowd immediately picked up the chant. Moments later, the entire coliseum shook, chanting his name. The old champion slowly crossed the finish line. He helped his dazed opponent down from the machine and followed him. Slowly and solemnly, he raised his right hand to the sky, his gaze following the tip of his fingers and continuing upward. The glory others bestowed on him at that moment, he passed on to someone else. How long he had waited for this moment. As a young man, amid all the applause he received, he would bow and proudly raise the

Champions' Cup. Now, with silvered hair and a wise heart, he looked upward and gave thanks to his Inspirer.

"What a beautiful end to a turbulent and glory-filled career!" Grace could not hold back.

But no one else seemed to hear her except Rock, who nodded in agreement, then resumed clapping with all his might.

After a final honorary lap of the "Galeus Stadium," Jadon Van Doeren entered the pits. The coliseum began to slowly empty. The sun had risen to its highest point, inviting everyone to seek a resting place in the shady covered restaurants and taverns.

The small squad of Captain Veren withdrew to one such modest tavern not far from the stadium, by the small lake about a kilometer from the site. There, under the mix of pleasant sounds from tambura and bagpipe and the fragrant local Galey dishes, the five crew members of the "Hunter" awaited their champion.

Although finishing last in the race, Jadon was the true winner today. With dancing and revelry until late into the night, they properly celebrated his victory. Several times, Rock couldn't resist and tossed his "professor-champion" into the air. Steven and Jeremy were thrilled to have the honor of flying with such a legendary figure. Grace, though not very understanding of these "men's things," was also caught up in the mood that filled her colleagues. The sun caressed the matte skin of her face, highlighting the beautiful blended features of the finest of two races.

Only Veren stood a little apart, thoughtful, probably contemplating upcoming events. But by late afternoon, he too relaxed and fully joined the celebration.

A CHANCE ENCOUNTER

At the moment when three new satellites, Yasef, Morgon, and Renie appeared in the starry sky, and the planet Eleal shone in all its splendor, the merry crew of the Hunter returned to their starship. Everyone knew this celebration might well be their last. Tomorrow awaited them with fierce battles and a brutal confrontation with the prince of the Air Dominion at the Yoke station. The Hunters had flown for one hundred and twenty hours when a small glowing dot appeared on the radar in the command room. "What is that!?" Grace jumped up from her chair. "It's still too distant to see through the viewport, but I'll check what the radar picked up," Verin replied. After a quick scan, the captain reported,

"It's a moving object on a trajectory about one hundred and fifty light-minutes from our starship. It's being followed by seven smaller moving units." Verin furrowed his brow, suspicion curling the thick eyebrow over his right eye.

"Grace, have the Hunters prepare for launch! Eleal's trading ships don't travel this far. The three warships of the Royal Squadron are to join us later. And those seven units? They look like shuttles from the Dark Royal forces. Ready the starship's guns!" ordered the captain. Within minutes, the crew was on high alert, each at their station, waiting. On the horizon, the detected object began to shimmer more clearly. "Hunter 2, 3, and 4, ready for launch!" Verin's voice crackled over the comms... "Zero!" The three Hunters shot into the void. The skayers formed a triangle and headed toward the increasingly visible object. They flew swiftly, closing in fast before them emerged a moderately sized spaceship, with seven shuttles clinging to it like leeches. "Captain, ahead is a ship in poor condition. The hull bears the name Seeker. The ship seems to be under siege by shuttles from the 'Fear' squadron," reported Steven, leader of the skayers. "Awaiting further orders!" Hunter gave the command to attack. The Hunters surged toward the unsuspecting enemy. Two of the shuttles exploded under the first volley. A dizzying chase began.

SEEKER

At one point, it was unclear who was chasing whom. Lasers from the enemy shuttles whistled like fireworks around the Hunters. With a swift maneuver, Hunter III and IV detached from Steven and launched their assault. Forming a line, they spun around their central companion like blades, eliminating three of the 'Fear' shuttles. The battle was brief — the last two royal machines exploded almost simultaneously, leaving only their wreckage drifting in space. "They destroyed them with enviable ease," the captain muttered to himself, watching the skayers return through the panoramic window. "My friend the Touched was right: I've been assigned some of the kingdom's finest pilots!" "Rock, what do you say? Shall we start the count?" Steven laughed through the radio. "Three to two in your favor, huh? The gauntlet's been thrown..." replied the dark-skinned giant in kind. Hunter was already near the site of the recently ended battle. The Seeker requested contact, and the two ships docked. Crossing the boarding bridge, lowered by Hunter, Verin, Ispulnen, and TR-di stepped aboard. The two men were fully armored, unsure of the intentions of the Seeker crew. Their weapons, bestowed by Eleal's chancellor, marked them as elite warriors—lightweight yet devastatingly effective. At the far end of the bridge, the main portal slid open. Against the hexagonal frame of the airlock stood a solitary human figure. Verin and Jadon cautiously stepped forward. The figure was unnaturally stooped, as if burdened by tons on his back. His face was clouded with despair and exhaustion. The younger Hunter took a step forward and introduced himself:

"I'm Captain Verin, commander of this starship called Hunter. We come bearing peaceful intentions on a special mission." Slowly, the man moved and, with effort, parted his lips, pointing a finger behind him. "Gentlemen, please come aboard. We hold no hostile intentions either." The Hunters and the robot followed their host. Along the way, they passed a few more people — men and women whose faces bore the same hopelessness and weariness. They were led to a cabin where three older men awaited them. Judging by their attire, these were the leaders of the Seeker. Verin and Jadon settled into comfortable chairs courteously offered. TR-di stood to Verin's left. Between them and the others lay a round mahogany table in the room's center. The cabin was cold, as was everywhere aboard the ship. Silence fell, broken at last by the eldest host. He rose slowly, leaning on the polished table with both hands. A small white beard framed his time-worn, deeply creased face. "My name is

Despair," he began awkwardly, "and these are Not Knowing and Confused." He gestured left and right. "We are the three commanders of Seeker. Under our leadership are five hundred and twenty men, women, and children who fled from the Yoke station." Verin's skin prickled. He and Jadon exchanged a meaningful glance. Despair seemed unaware of the reaction his words stirred and continued in the same monotonous tone: "We escaped the dictator regime of the Dark Kings, whose shuttles you destroyed moments ago. We wanted to leave this cursed place behind. But our plan failed as we had feared. We have been relentlessly pursued and monitored. For ten years we've wandered this system, unable to break free from the curse's grasp." "Do you know where you're headed? Do you know the way?" Jadon asked, not averting his gaze from the weary commander's heavy eyelids. "Do I know? I no longer believe we will ever leave the Kozela system. Many years ago, at Yoke, there was an old man. His ancestors were pilgrims who told him of a Kingdom with a merciful ruler who gathered his people like a shepherd. He gathered them from all corners of the universe, scattered and enslaved by the prince of the Air Dominion. He even gave his own son as a ransom for the lost. We believed in that story then. Today, we don't know what to believe, what we do, or where we are going." The old man lifted his eyes, heavy tears slipping down his pale, ghostly face. "Are you the only ones who escaped?" the captain of the Hunter asked quickly. "We escaped on two ships, ours and a larger one called Deceived, but their crew lost all hope and returned to Yoke. We heard nothing more of them. Every day, I expect my people to rebel and wish to return. To be honest, that thought is not alien to me either." Silence hung in the air. "We have been sent by the Kingdom," Verin declared firmly. The three exchanged glances. Their faces remained cloaked in sorrow, but moments later, their expressions sharpened, eyes glowing with eager focus on the young captain. "Son, I am old. Please, do not mock my tormented soul..." Despair sighed. "There truly is such a place. A Kingdom of justice and peace, mercy and understanding. Its one and eternal ruler is the King of kings. He governs with truth and love, cherishing His subjects deeply. He calls us His sons." The three listened with mouths agape, greedily drinking in Verin's words. Doubt and hope flickered in their eyes, locked in a relentless battle. Somewhere deep in the hearts of these weary seekers, faith began to rise from the ruins of despair. "Sir, will you enter the coordinates into our ship's computer? I don't know you, but your words have stirred this old heart again. Show us the way, dear sir!" The seeker's voice trembled. "We will input the coordinates. Your quest has already paved the path among the stars to the Kingdom. It is already in your hearts," Verin answered without hesitation. Suddenly, the cold seemed to leave the cabin. Life pulsed anew. The Hunters followed their hosts to the ship's command center. There, TR-di uploaded the coordinates to the Mercy Cloud and the planet Eleal. "From today and forevermore, you are members of the Kingdom. Your journey there will be fraught with many obstacles and far from easy, but I urge you to keep going and never give up!" Jadon concluded with a smile just before they left the Seeker. About half an hour later, the two ships separated and continued on their paths. Seeker, along with its crew, changed not only citizenship but also their names, now reflecting their new homeland. Thus, the new Discoverer soared toward its longed-for land. Moments later, the mega thrusters ignited, and the Hunter jumped into hyperspace.

THE LEAP

"From this moment on, we must be extremely cautious!" Veran had gathered the crew of the Hunter in the ship's command hall. "We're too close to the Dark Kings' station now. They've surely detected the explosion of their own shuttles and are likely investigating. Around 20:30, our radars registered an unknown presence at 45. 35 degrees to our right. I urge you all to remain on high alert. Report to this command center via your personal transmitters every twenty minutes! You'll speak to me or Grace. Be ready for an alarm! The enemy does not sleep but prowls like a roaring lion, seeking whom it may devour." After receiving their orders, the hunters left the room. The Hunter adjusted its course. To the left of their initial trajectory lay a small asteroid, once called Grace. It had once served as a rest and recovery base for travelers and merchants, a haven under the Kingdom's protection—until it was abandoned and desolated by the forces of the Air Prince. Veran had chosen it as their landing site to prepare for the upcoming assault. Afterward, they would wait in orbit for the three ships of the Royal Fleet arriving from the Gavaon constellation.

Two hours later, the Hunter touched down on the asteroid's surface. "What devastation!" "Yes, Grace," Veran replied. "To think this place once welcomed weary travelers… The presence of the Dark Kings leaves nothing untouched." "It must have been beautiful, a warm, inviting place. What happened to it?" Grace asked, her voice trembling slightly. "As I said, the inhabitants and guests of the asteroid—your namesake—lived in peace and harmony until the Dark Kings arrived. Disguised as royal envoys of light, they deceived the local government. They brought promises of a 'new order,' claiming to speak on behalf of the King. Grace's people, unsuspecting and naive, handed over control to the so-called 'New Government.' From that day on, they lost their freedom. The land withered, stripped of beauty and vitality. The air itself vanished. We'll need our suits." Through the panoramic window, the hunters gazed upon deserted buildings, crumbling runways, and the skeletal remains of what were once lush gardens, waterfalls, and fountains. Charred, rotting tree trunks jutted from the cracked ground, casting a ghostly image over the ruined landscape.

For the next three hours, every system on the Hunter was checked. Anti-air laser cannons were readied. Rocket bays were stocked. The rear sector—housing crew quarters, storage, and the now-empty cargo hold—was detached, making the ship faster and more agile. "Jadon... Jadon... respond!" Veran's voice echoed through the intercom. "We need to prepare for launch." Jadon, the professor, had been missing for about twenty minutes. Steven and Rock went looking for him and quickly found him perched atop a crumbling wall. Soon after, the Hunter lifted off, rising two thousand meters above the surface before cutting its engines to wait for the other ships. "Professor, were you out on an archaeological dig in Grace?" Jeremy teased as the crew walked down the illuminated corridor toward the lab of Ispulen to discuss their tactical plans. Jadon, who usually welcomed jokes, didn't respond. "You alright, Professor?" asked the short, dark-haired young man, now serious. Jadon gave a weak shrug and forced a smile. "No problem," he said curtly and hurried ahead to open the lab. The hunters gathered around a large star map at the center of the room. Veran stood in its middle and addressed them. "Gentlemen," he began. "We've been entrusted with the responsibility and the privilege to lead the battle for Eden, now known as 'Yoke.' Only our squad will breach the station's heart as the assault unit. The three other starships, along with the Hunter, will strike from the outside." He pointed to the map. "Here lies the command nexus, the fallen prince's throne room. Four corridors lead to it, all heavily guarded. We'll use this one on the right, it's the least protected. But first, we need to seize one of the side runways—Runway Six—our allies from the Explorer confirmed it's the least patrolled. "Steven and Jeremy, you'll launch a frontal assault, flying at 23 degrees to the Hunter's right. Rock will depart half an hour earlier, circle around the station with all transceivers off to remain undetected, and land on Runway Two, where there are only transport ships and little combat presence. "Meanwhile, I'll land with Hunter One and capture the radar installations on the command mast. Our ship, along with the three cruisers, will bombard the main runway to draw enemy fire." Veran turned to Jadon and Grace.

"You'll stay aboard with the droid. Your task: damage the runway as much as possible to prevent enemy launches. Then stay in orbit and cover us." "Sounds too easy," the professor muttered. "The vision of a united and restored Kingdom of Eden will inspire our hearts and strengthen our hands to prevail," Veran replied calmly. "And if the plan fails?" Jadon pressed. "They'll spot the Hunter immediately." "They will—but they'll sweat trying to track us. By then, we'll already be in a position. And now… let me reveal one of our ship's secrets. Back on Galea, not only did they sync our cannons, they also installed fifth-generation electronic camouflage." "Never heard of such a thing," Jadon interrupted harshly. "You'll hear now," Veran said, his brow narrowing. "This tech will render us nearly invisible—but only for thirty-five minutes. After that, our visibility rapidly increases. So we'll have just over half an hour to complete all preparations. Only we, as the landing craft, have the Chameleon SDR system. The cruisers will remain one mini-parsec behind us, laying covering fire." "Understood," the professor muttered, retreating from the map and dropping heavily into a chair, tossing a small ball from hand to hand. "These digital trackers are linked to the Hunter's computer. They'll guide your coordinates," Veran continued, pointing to four devices on the control table.

"Now, let us step forward into battle as true warriors of the Kingdom!" he declared. The hunters knelt, joined hands, and lifted their faces to the dome above. Silence fell over the room. Minutes later, they rose—only to discover the professor was gone. It was a fact that finally unleashed Veran's growing concern.

"What's happened to Jadon?" Rock asked, puzzled.

"Something's rotten here!" the captain growled. "This doesn't feel right..." He furrowed his brow.

"I felt it too," Grace added thoughtfully. At that moment, Steven's voice called out from behind.

At that moment, Steven's voice called out from behind.

"Captain, one of the digital seekers is missing!" A sense of dread surged through Veran and Rock, and they bolted out the door toward the command deck. The corridor was empty—no sign of Jadon. Rock's long strides took him ahead of Veran, and he was the first to storm into Hunter-I. Inside, he found the professor activating the transmitter. "Jadon, what are you doing?" Rock's eyes narrowed with suspicion. Moments later, Veran appeared, thermal blade in hand. Van Doeren jumped to his feet, blaster aimed at them. A shot rang out, slamming into the wall just above their heads. The black giant lunged at the attacker, but the man twisted sharply and fired again. Rock cried out—his shoulder drenched in blood. The barrel of the blaster pressed against his temple. "Don't move or I'll blow his brains out!" Van Doeren snarled, his voice guttural, more like a rabid dog's bark than anything human. Veran could hardly believe it was the professor speaking. "You sound like a pack of rabid hounds. Who are you really?" Veran demanded. Rock lay motionless on the floor, the blaster at his head. With effort, he curled his lip into a grin and hissed through his teeth:

"Captain, don't spare him! This one's from the dark side. That's not Jadon. Van Doeren is a hero—this thing's a wretch." The impostor cursed viciously. Veran struck. The intruder was forced to swing the blaster away from Rock and aim at his attacker. He fired. But Veran intercepted the shot mid-air with his thermal blade. Another blast. The captain dove aside just in time. Then, with a crash, the fake Jadon fell face-first to the ground. Rock had swept his legs from beneath him, then brought his heel crashing down on the impostor's back. The "professor" moved no more. His body began to fade, becoming translucent, and then melted into a puddle of foul, gelatinous slime. "That was a dark lord," Veran said, rising to his feet. "Rock, are you badly hurt?" The wounded man gave the captain a bewildered look, then nodded faintly. "We ran into something like this about two years ago," Rock said, gritting his teeth as Veran helped him up. "I couldn't believe my eyes back then, but I learned—our enemy can mimic even the brightest of angels. Careful not to get any of that filth on you." "He didn't manage to transmit anything," Veran confirmed, casting a glance over the control panel. "We got here just in time. And here's the digital seeker—still on the chair. The agent jumped the gun—I hadn't even loaded the data yet. Ha!" Despite the pain in his shoulder, Rock laughed. At that moment, Jadon appeared at the door, TR-DI right behind him.

"Hey, guys—looks like I missed something!" he grinned with his usual cheer. "Seems like you missed me a little." The two men chuckled.

"Jadon, what the hell happened?" Rock asked, almost in tears. "Where were you?" He tried to sound serious. Then he grabbed the outstretched hand of the newcomer and squeezed it so tightly that Jadon almost cried out. "Just making sure you're the real deal. Nothing personal." "What happened, friend?" Veran added. "Your double nearly gave us heart attacks." "Let the others gather, and I'll tell you all. You might learn something from what happened to me." Minutes later, the crew of the Hunter assembled in the command room. "How did they manage to replace you, Professor?" "No one's immune to that, dear brother Jeremy," Jadon replied. "Believe me, I'll wear this lesson like an earring. And I hope none of you ever go through the same." "But what did happen?" Steven blurted out. "When we landed on Gracefall and started prepping the starship, I took a minute to look around. I'd heard stories of the beauty of this asteroid. Curiosity got the better of me. I saw a small, nearly dried-up spring and sat down on a rock nearby. What I didn't realize was that the rock was one of those so-called 'Charmstones' scientists write about. The moment I sat down, my head spun—and I fell asleep. When I woke up, a small scout shuttle from the Dark Order was nearby. I nearly screamed in terror—standing before me was… me." Jadon chuckled at the memory. "They must have scanned my bio-signature and created a perfect copy. Then two of them tied me up and smuggled me aboard Hunter. They shoved me into a ventilation shaft. That's when you all noticed I was missing. The rest—you know." The crew sat around Jadon, their gazes fixed on the floor. "The moral of the story," he said, "is to always be where you're supposed to be—and do your duty. I apologize to all of you for the danger I put you in. Forgive me, my friends." Jadon slumped into a seat. Over the next half hour, the crew conducted a thorough sweep of the starship. They searched everything. To their relief, nothing else seemed suspicious. The team returned to their posts, awaiting the arrival of the Royal Destroyers.

CLASH AMONG THE STARS

Seventy-one hours later, three bright blips lit up the radar. Reinforcements had arrived. Massive and imposing, the cruisers would provide powerful cover and a solid rear guard. But the task of striking at the heart of the enemy remained the sole responsibility of the Hunters. The battle group entered the border zone of "Ygo." The radar remained eerily silent—no signs of movement. "Prepare the skyers for launch!" came Veren's voice through the ship's comms. "We proceed as planned!" From the deck of the Hunter, Grace was tasked with coordinating the cruisers' fire, masking the launch of the Hunter's skyers.

Half an hour later, a colossal orbital station appeared on the radar display. Spindle-shaped and encircled by a massive ring, it slowly rotated along its orbit, growing larger with every passing second. "How are we feeling, boys? Think we'll make it?" the captain's voice crackled in the pilots' earpieces. "We'll see what those guys inside are made of," replied Rock. "I've never quit without at least taking a shot." "First time facing something like this. But we'll crush them. They're in for a beating!" Jeremy growled over the comm. "I don't know about you, but I plan on leaving those bastards with nightmares," Steven chimed in. "Glad to hear the spirit's high!" the captain laughed. "Now go get 'em—and remember who's stronger." It was Rock's turn to launch. With a sharp command, Hunter-3 shot toward Ygo's left sector. Thanks to his exceptional piloting, he reached "Runway-2" undetected by the station's security systems and patrol shuttles. He landed on the vacant pad and waited for further instructions. Hunter-2 and -4 followed, and finally Veren launched in Hunter-1. Jadon, Grace, and TR-D remained in the starship's lab, managing its systems and maintaining contact with the Royal Cruisers. "I think we've been spotted," reported the professor, eyes fixed on the glowing monitor. "Grace, tell Rock to abandon his skyer and seize control of the runway tower!"

Seconds later, the Hunter erupted with fire, targeting an enemy squadron moving in fast. The three other ships opened fire in unison. The enemy's advance halted instantly. Redirecting its fire, the Hunter now assaulted "Runway-1," where the bulk of the enemy fleet was stationed. A chaotic weave of fiery beams tangled the space between them. Then, three heavily armed Destroyers locked onto the Hunter. "Professor, we need to maneuver—we're on a collision course!" Grace cried out, her eyes wide with alarm. "If we try to dodge, we'll expose our flank or take a hit from behind. Our front shields are the strongest—we can absorb a salvo or two." The veteran hunter remained calm, a calm that soothed even Grace. "Input the coordinates to the cruisers—tell them to open fire. Now!" The professor's order was obeyed immediately. Grace transferred the data to the three cruisers. In the next moment, a massive explosion shook the Hunter's hull. A blinding light consumed the viewport. Jadon, who had been standing near the glass, was thrown back into the wall. "I'm alright..." he groaned. "Open the missile bays! Fire two Faith rockets!"

Without hesitation, Grace locked onto the leading Destroyer and slammed the red button. Two fiery rockets hissed out, colliding with brutal force. A blinding flash washed over the battlefield—then nothing. The Destroyer had vanished. A swarm of debris scattered like bees in space. The three Royal Cruisers finished the job, obliterating the remaining two ships. "We survived!" the professor grinned as he climbed back into his seat. "That went well." "Our front shield's down to twenty percent. Another hit like that, and we'll be wreckage." "You're right. Rotate thirty degrees to starboard—we've got fifty percent shielding there." "Will we make it?" Grace asked, doubt flickering in her eyes. "We'll win this fight," Jadon replied, his gaze locked on hers—calm, unshakable. And she believed him.

Seconds later, the starship began its rotation, presenting its left side to the station. The silenced cannons thundered back to life, unleashing a new storm on their deadly target. A violent blast followed by a flash of searing light hurled Rock several meters across the tarmac. The next thing he saw was a pair of bare feet. He tried to push himself up, but a sharp pain in his shoulder kept him on the ground. Gritting his teeth, he gathered his strength. With a hiss of pain escaping his clenched jaw, he stood. The moment felt like an eternity. How long had he been lying here? And who was standing before him now? The first question was swept aside by the second. Instinctively, the hunter reached for the sword at his belt. "The three cruisers are gone..." a coarse male voice growled above him—in a language Rock hadn't heard in years. "Your weaponry is... formidable." "Edenic," Rock muttered slowly, regaining his balance. "That tongue hasn't been spoken in centuries..." Ето художествения превод на откъса на английски: "...But you speak it quite well," the stranger went on. "Yes. I do," the hunter narrowed his eyes and studied the man standing before him. "I studied it at the Academy. And you—who are you?" The stranger straightened his shoulders slightly and pulled the hood of his robe back with his right hand. A weathered, time-carved face appeared, with two lifelessly pale eyes. Long white hair spilled down either side of his head and fell heavily onto his shoulders. "I am Edreal—the Watcher. I come from the City of the Doomed." "But the City of the Doomed is far from this airstrip. It lies at the heart of Yoke. What are you doing here?" The hunter's tone grew sharp, suspicion seeping into his mind like a creeping fog. The man before him seemed harmless—just an old, blind wretch. But what was he doing here? Could he be a scout for the Dark Ones? According to Intel, Runway-2 was supposed to be abandoned… "Do not fear," the old man cut off the growing storm in his mind.

"As long as I can remember, this place has always been deserted. This half-ruined little strip holds no interest for the Station Governor. Something I've taken advantage of for many years." "And… what exactly are you doing here?" Rock asked again. "I was waiting for you." "For us?!" the dark-skinned warrior nearly shouted. "I saw your ship one hundred and twenty years ago. Back then, I was young—like you…" "Well, now you've lost me," the hunter shrugged. "How could you have seen us? You can't even see me now…" "You can take your hand off your sword. That red suit suits your skin tone perfectly." Rock awkwardly lowered his hand from the hilt. Who was this strange man? "Forget the idea of storming the control tower. A full squad of elite Dark troops is stationed there. Follow me. I'll lead you to the tower's generator. From there, your mission will be much easier."

"But how do you know…?" Actually, questions now seemed pointless. Nothing made sense anymore. Yet deep inside, Rock felt a calm certainty that he should follow this blind stranger. Besides, the blast had knocked him out for nearly nine minutes. "I don't have time to fight a whole squad. I'll trust you and come." "I see you lack neither courage nor sense," Edreal smiled, his aged face lighting up with warm sincerity. "Come." Rock said nothing. He had no choice but to trust the odd blind man and accept his invitation. Apparently, the explosion had also knocked out communications. "The plan's a bust," the hunter growled to himself. "Sometimes a lost battle doesn't mean the war is lost," Edreal said, without even turning around. The old man walked slowly but with purpose, occasionally steadying himself with a long, thin staff. They crossed the desolate strip and entered a dim, half-lit corridor. Overhead, dangling wires, cracked pipes, and strips of peeling paint hung like cobwebs. The air was damp, and here and there their boots splashed through shallow puddles. A swarm of questions buzzed through Rock's head, mingling with the rhythmic tap of Edreal's staff and the irritating drip from above. They turned right, then passed through more corridors—each one more eerie than the last, enough to raise the hair on any living man's neck. "We're here," the Edemian broke the ghostly silence. "This is it?" Rock asked skeptically. "You're telling me this tiny box powers the whole tower?"

"It's only a relay node, but it'll do. Afterward, we can restore it easily and make use of the airstrip." "Make use of the strip?…" That was, in fact, part of the hunters' goal, but what exactly did this old man mean? "We're leaving the base, aren't we?" "We are." With that, the giant warrior drew his sword and, with two swift strikes, shattered the square relay device and everything inside it. "That's enough. The tower is now without power," Edreal said calmly. "Now, follow me." Rock trailed silently behind the bent figure of the elder. It was strange how easily the Edemian had won his trust. They passed through a few more corridors, then suddenly the rusted ceiling gave way. Above them stretched a sky of dark, gray clouds. Beneath the gloomy veil, hundreds—thousands of lights outlined the shape of a sprawling city. Several tall towers pierced the leaden sky like ancient titans, holding it aloft. "The city…" "The City of the Doomed," Edreal finished. "Our fate…" "Fate. Hmph!

We'll see about that." "Many are ready to follow you, stranger," the old man turned to him. "The ancient prophecies speak of you and your companions. We, the doomed, want to change our fate. And you must help us." Rock said nothing. This old Edemian kept surprising him.

"Our ancestors left signs and writings on several ancient mounds at the city's edge. They speak of eagles from the Southern Star, who will take us from the nest of the doomed and carry us to the Mighty Rock. Only from Runway 2 can the Southern Star be seen." "Do you believe these writings?" the hunter asked seriously. Edreal straightened, supporting his back with one hand. A heavy sigh escaped his lips. "Believe? I live to see those prophetic words fulfilled. As absurd as it may sound—for someone who cannot see," he chuckled. "And where are those mounds?" "We hide them. The Dark Ones must not find them." "I'd like to see them, but I have to hurry. Our intel was wrong—the strip is completely empty. I don't know if the rest of our parameters are off, too. Either way, I have to reach Yoke's central node—fast."

"I'll take you. Follow me," Edreal said simply, setting off at the fastest pace he could manage. They entered the city streets. Rock asked no more questions—he had decided to fully trust the Edemian Watcher. Not that he had much of a choice. The gray stares of passersby seemed to swallow him whole. Hatred, envy, and fear clung to the place like poisoned darts, trying to pierce his armored chest and sap his strength. Rock paused. Took a deep breath. And moved on. The hurried crowd flowed around them like a rushing river, threatening to sweep them away. Towering glass buildings loomed like giants. One could still see the elegant touch of the Edenite architect who had once shaped this city. But centuries of darkness and slavery had eroded much of its beauty. "Don't these people know there's a war outside?"

"They have no idea," Edreal replied quickly. "To them, this metropolis is everything. They believe they're the center of the universe. But they don't even realize they're prisoners inside a nightmarish base of the Dark Lords." Soon they emerged onto a small cobbled square, its design a relic of a long-forgotten century. "Old man, I need to find my team. Take me to the station's control node," Rock removed his helmet and ran a restless hand through his dark curls. "I hope the boys are okay!" "We need to cross the district, then we'll reach the forbidden sectors. In about twenty minutes, I can gather the Initiated. They'll take you wherever you need to go—and help you. You can trust them completely." "Do you think they're up to it? These are elite imperial troops we're facing." Edreal slowly removed his hood and turned his lifeless gaze toward his companion. "These men and women have trained their whole lives for this moment. Their fathers, mothers, and grandparents believed and lived, trained and sacrificed for a time such as this. They waved at their dream from afar—but never saw it. Now their children have a chance to change their fate. I have no doubt they'll seize it. All they need… is someone to lead them." The old man's face glowed with passion. "Lead me. I trust you…"

His words were cut off by a powerful explosion. One of the buildings behind him collapsed. Millions of fragments rained down on the square. The beautiful fountain at its center was buried. Rock threw himself over Edreal, shielding him with his body. Several heavy stones slammed into his back shield. The dark-skinned warrior shook off the shock and rose, only to be struck again. A thermal bullet glanced off his helmet with a screech. Then a hailstorm of energy fire rained down on them. Spinning, Rock unfastened the shield from his back and held it in front of them both. The thermal rounds hammered the oval slab of Nubilium, but they remained safe beneath it. Rock stole a glance ahead—fire came from both corners. Dozens of enemies, maybe more. "We're surrounded..." the giant roared over the din. "They've cut off every way out!" Edreal said nothing. His face was unnaturally calm. The shield still held, but Rock's arms began to tremble.

Holding the cover with his left hand, he drew his sword with the right. If he just stayed there, they'd be crushed by the thermal barrage. So he decided to attack—probably a suicidal move, but better than waiting to die. He hoped to draw the fire away long enough for Edreal to escape. "Old man, I'm leaving you. If you can—run! Don't wait for me..." were the hunter's final words. Then he sprang up and charged toward his unseen enemies. He veered left—fire seemed weaker there. With a quick spin of his shield, he deflected a central blast. His blade knocked aside a few more shots. Then another volley slammed into his shield. A sharp pain in his chest dropped him. He nearly blacked out. His chestplate was crushed, warped, but not pierced. The fire didn't stop. It grew even fiercer. Voices shouted. The battle raged, shifting deeper into the buildings. What was happening? Was he still alive? The pain said yes. Were they attacking the old man now? Rock didn't know. He lay pinned behind his shield, barely breathing. Then—silence. The shouting ceased. The weapons fell quiet.

Through the transparent shield, Rock saw a young man step into view. The stranger knelt and lifted the protective dome. "Are you all right, warrior? Can you move?" he asked. "Give me a hand and I'll answer that," the hunter reached out. "Who are you?" "My name is Worthy. I'm with the Initiated. We took out a whole Dark platoon. But we need to move—now."

THE HEART OF "YOKE"

After a fierce firefight with the anti-aircraft guns of "Runway-6," Steven and Jeremy had managed to land and abandon their skarriers. From there, they infiltrated the corridors of the station with ease. Verin had already taken control of the command mast and its radar systems and was now headed toward the power core. The three hunters—minus Rock—rendezvoused at one of the branching junctions of the corridor maze. According to the plan, this was where they were supposed to wait for him. "He's still not here! His transmitter is off," Verin noted, glancing at his timer. "We have to go without him. Switching to backup plan."

A sigh, barely audible, broke the firmness of his voice for a fleeting second. "May the King's mercy be upon him." Jeremy and Steven silently followed their commander. They knew that no matter how much their hearts ached, they had to press on. At that moment, they were caught between the hammer and the anvil—and any delay might doom the mission. And it was precisely for that mission that Rock may have sacrificed his life. The corridors toward the core trembled with the roar of weapons and the savage howls of chaos. Heavily armed patrols scoured the station, hunting the intruders. Twice, the hunters clashed with enemy units in close skirmishes, each time erasing them completely before vanishing like shadows. Confusion deepened among the "dark forces" when two thunderous explosions shook the station. The King's destroyers, led by the Hunter, had once again made their presence known. A third explosion threw them all to the floor. Then came a sickening slide and the screech of tearing metal—the last strike had likely knocked Yoke out of orbit and ruptured one of its polar shields. Shaking off the shock, the hunters pressed forward, fast and unseen. Their suits rendered them invisible to the station's defense sensors. But as they emerged into a more open area, they stumbled into an ambush. The large platform lit up with a hail of gunfire.

Verin and Steven were struck down by the initial barrage, but their chest plates held, sparing their lives. Jeremy remained standing, shielding them both with his barrier. The enemy charged like a hurricane. Despite the chaos, Verin and Steven managed to get back on their feet. "Form a circle! Defensive formation!" Verin shouted, his voice nearly lost in the rising thunder. In the face of impossible odds, the three aligned back-to-back, each guarding the others. From all sides, armored dark soldiers poured in, their thermal beams slamming into the hunters' shields, helmets, and armor. The air quivered from the rising heat. Inhuman shrieks pierced the space around them, threatening to steal their breath. "The weapons are holding… just don't give up… don't give up!" Verin's voice rasped through the firestorm. Then, silence—the battle's roar drowned him once more. The "dark ones" had pushed the trio into the platform's edge when suddenly a blaze of red fire burst behind the attackers—a flaming sword! Rock had emerged from the shadows, tearing through enemy ranks like a tempest.

With powerful blows, he brought chaos to the tight-knit enemy lines. A thunderous battle cry erupted behind him— dozens of unfamiliar men and women followed at his back, fearless and relentless. Suddenly, silence fell again. Only the clash of blades and the sizzle of blasters echoed. "Attack!" Verin bellowed. The three-cornered hunters surged into the fray. Their swords spun so fast they seemed like burning discs. Now it was the dark soldiers who were trapped. Disoriented, they scattered and fled. "Don't let them escape!" Rock called to one of the Edenites. "Then return to the city and help Edreal arm all the Awakened!" Within minutes, the battlefield was cleared. Charred remnants of the fallen lay scattered. At the center, the hunters stood still, watching the dying echoes of the fight. "Let's move to the core. We don't have much time," Verin's voice sounded once more.

At the same time, the dark forces were suffering heavy losses from the King's artillery, led by the starship Hunter. Yoke's fleet had been severely reduced, now relying only on scattered defensive fire. But at any moment, the Hunter would become a visible target. Its camouflage was faltering. Three shots from Yoke had already slammed into its shield. "The generators still hold enough power to keep the shield up far longer than the cloak," the professor said to Grace. "Let's hope it lasts. If not, we'll need to pull back to the

Angelic Destroyers' line," she replied without taking her eyes off the control panel. Suddenly, her brow furrowed and her gaze sharpened. "What is it?" Jadon asked. "I don't know… sensors on the port side are picking up something…" "Something?" "A foreign object. Looks like it's stuck near our engine," Grace bit her lip.

"I have to check it out!" In the next second, she leapt from her chair and began fastening the straps of her holsters. "Might be a boarding team. One of those hits wasn't thermal. No shield's been invented yet that can stop that kind of intrusion." "Could be. I'll be careful. Keeping coms open. I'm taking TR-Di," she nodded. "You'd better," the old hunter said as she slammed her blasters into place. Van Doeren pressed a button on the console, sealing the hatch behind her. The starship's firepower had to continue, at all costs. The hunters on Yoke depended on that cover. Together with the robot, Grace raced through the corridors toward the signal. If the intruders had made it aboard, their counterattack could doom the mission—and the fate of every Edenite on Yoke. She stopped only at the end of the third branching hallway. Standing before the engine bay hatch, she drew her blasters. Her sword rested on her back, reserved for the final moment, if it came to that. TR-Di input the data into the code lock and opened the door. Grace crouched, leveling her blasters into the unknown. She peeked inside.

A breath of relief slipped from her lips—everything seemed fine. She stepped inside slowly, but a strange sensation overtook her. Something she couldn't name yet. A few meters into the dim chamber, she froze. A dark figure stood before her. No weapon in hand, but that didn't ease her tension. The boarding party had already infiltrated Hunter. And something deeper, darker began to churn in her chest. Grace aimed at the figure, fingers tightening on the triggers—until his voice stopped her cold. "Hello, Bitter One!" — the "Dark" broke the silence. — "Better look both ways before you make any move." The girl relaxed her triggers but didn't even think of lowering her blasters. She turned her head left and right and saw a "Dark" on each side, weapons trained on her. "No one has called me that in years!" — she answered boldly — "My name is Grace!" "Good. Since you're so into your new role — Grace it is," the stranger sneered with a disgusting voice. "Why don't you shoot?" "We could do that." "What do you want from me?" "First, I want you to remember who you were." "And who was that?!" — the girl growled. "You were one of our best fighters. The Prince had big plans for you. And, truth be told, he still does. That's why I'm here, and why you haven't been burned by my men's fire." "I knew it," Grace smiled coldly. "Trying to recruit me, Major Must?" "You could say that," came the invader's mocking laugh. "You had a lot of power in our camp. Now, who are you? Come back to us! Give us the secret codes, and you'll be crowned with more power and glory than ever!"

"'Glory and power'?" — the lady repeated thoughtfully. "I don't think I need them." "Everyone wants them. And you had plenty." "But at the cost of losing my soul... Actually, why am I even explaining this to you? If you're going to shoot—shoot! I won't give myself to you easily." "Look, your past wasn't all glory. You did many things your people wouldn't be proud of. Those deeds will hang around your neck like a millstone. Always dragging you down. And by the way, as a halfbreed between the black and white races, rejected by your own kind, we took you in. Allowed you to be one of us." — The major's voice betrayed him: — "And we know every one of your sins."

For a moment, silence fell in the dimness. A heavy silence that perhaps weighed the fate of two kingdoms. Grace closed her eyes. Shame from her past seemed to choke her breath again. Her cheeks and neck must have already been flushed. She really had done many dark deeds before. Things that now made her want to sink into the earth. She reflected on what the major had so helpfully reminded her of. Yes — until a few years ago, she was one of the elite officers in the imperial forces. As the daughter of a general, she had many privileges she could no longer claim. Colonel Bitter — that's how they addressed her. She commanded the Tenth Squadron of the Soulless. Often rejected by her own kind. Cast aside and despised for her mixed origin. Now she had no rank and was only an assistant commander on a starship. Strange — until now, she hadn't looked at things from this angle... The former "Soulless" bent her knees. She spread her arms as if to place her blasters on the floor. Bowed her head in a nod.

"It didn't take you long to reconsider," Major Must laughed smugly. The girl said nothing. She remained silent. But in the next moment, her pistols spoke. Actually, she had spread her arms to strike the two on her sides. She had crouched to be a harder target. She bowed her head to discreetly survey the scene. The two blasters joined as one before her, aiming at the third invader — the tempter. "Actually, my name is Grace! This Bitter One you speak of—I don't know her. I felt despised and rejected, but I hadn't yet found the love of My Father — the Creator, the Maker... I discovered I have wonderful, irreplaceable friends who accept me as I am. 'The old has passed away, behold, all things have become new!'" — The pistols fired, and the ghostly silhouette of the past collapsed silently to the floor. No second shot was needed — she never missed.

"I belong to another kingdom now! I definitely don't think I was wrong." A little later, the seemingly fragile woman walked calmly into the command room of the starship "Hunter." In her eyes, the professor could read only calm and strong confidence. Her beautiful matte complexion, typical of mulattos, radiated the assurance and peace of a beloved daughter. "What happened? I expected you to contact me." "Nothing special, just a brief meeting with my past. Everything is fine." "Yes, sometimes we all have those meetings." A gentle, fatherly smile appeared on Van Doeren's face. He looked at her understandingly, then returned his attention to the onboard computer. The four hunters proceeded on the marked route to the station's core. But there awaited another surprise...

Suddenly, behind their backs hissed an opening hatch. The corridor behind them had apparently closed. The air began to tremble and gray as the four vanished into the thick gloom. At that moment, something seemed to sit upon their chests, suffocating them. Their breathing grew difficult, and their eyes started to sting. Veren quickly recalled that section on the map, but it was already too late! He had planned to skip this stretch of the route. How could he have forgotten such an important detail? This was the corridor of the "Dark Shadow." Gradually, the hunters' arms and legs weakened, and one by one they began to collapse onto the floor. The dense veil had fully covered them. The warriors stared for an exit ahead, but not even millimeters of sight were possible.

Somewhere from the corridor's end came a thin, sinister voice, growing louder with every repetition and sounding more terrifying: "You are alone and abandoned! The Power you hoped for is gone!" Chills ran down the hunters' spines. The voice invoked feelings of loneliness and despair in their souls. Soon, the four were completely overcome by these feelings. Nearby echoed heavy footsteps. The hunters sensed a foreign, chilling presence. In the darkness came a snap. Something like heavy shackles locked their wrists. Similar bonds fastened their feet. "All is lost! The mission is over!" — a strong thought echoed in the captain's mind. Veren let his arms fall, his head bowed forward. His body also began to agree with what was happening around.

"Without entering the command center and dethroning the prince, the starship and the cruisers will be crushed by the rest of the enemy armada. Maybe someone else, maybe sometime in the future, will fulfill the King's Command for this doomed station." Veren slumped to the floor and sat down. "This cannot be the end!" — these words began to pierce through the thick cloud of despair in his mind — "It cannot all end like this!" — thoughts crept through his blurred mind. Then, like a clear stream, came another thought that refreshed him and made him shiver. Several verses from the Holy Edenic Book began to fill him: "Praise be to the King shall be on their lips, a sharp sword in both their hands, to execute vengeance on the nations and punishment on the peoples; to bind their kings with chains and their nobles with fetters of iron; to carry out the written judgment." Then Veren sang: "The Lord is my shepherd; I shall not want. He makes me lie down in green pastures; He leads me beside still waters. He restores my soul; He leads me in paths of righteousness for His name's sake."

The other three hunters joined their captain: "Yea, though I walk through the valley of the shadow of death, I will fear no evil, for You are with me; Your rod and Your staff, they comfort me." A warm wave flooded the four men. A feeling of peace and security filled their hearts. The gray fog began to vanish as quickly as it had appeared. They

could now see freely through their helmet visors. And then...
once more, breath caught in their chests. Before them stood
a three-meter giant, with their broken shackles lying at his
feet. The giant was clad in heavy armor. In his hands, he
held a massive thermal sword. "You, insignificant little
creatures!" — he growled fearfully. — "You made it this far,
but now I will end your mission." "Who are you?" — Veren
asked calmly, trying not to show his feelings. "I am General
Blasphemer. Warlord of 'Yoke'." — the giant snarled in
reply. The hunters slowly drew their swords from their
sheaths and gripped their shields tighter.

"As far as I understand, you are tasked with the insane
mission to destroy the principality of 'Yoke.' But here you
will meet your death! Loathsome royal servants! I challenge
one of you to a duel!" His red eyes stopped challengingly
on each hunter with undisguised disgust and contempt.
Jeremy stepped forward without hesitation. "I'll fight you!"
— he declared. "You?!" — Blasphemer pointed at the bulky
Rock, who, like the others, had also prepared to step
forward to fight. "No, I'll be the one!" — Jeremy stated firmly.
— "And since you threw contempt and blasphemy at the

King and his servants with your big mouth, you'll pay dearly for that!" Jeremy swung provocatively at the general. "You, little madman..." — Blasphemer barked angrily, visibly irritated by the hunter's words and actions. — "I'll crush you like an insect!" "General, I see you're better at talking..." — Jeremy laughed. — "You stand against me in your own strength, but I come in the Name of the King, against whom you cast contempt!" — the hunter shouted. Jeremy jumped aside to avoid Blasphemer's charging blade, which plunged into the metal corridor wall. A shower of sparks rained onto the hunters' shields. Jeremy rolled forward swiftly, grabbing a pair of broken shackles. He stood and swung them overhead. The shackles whistled through the air and struck Blasphemer's helmet. The general tried to keep balance but collapsed, shaking the entire corridor under his weight. His body was truly enormous.

Immediately, he began to liquefy until he turned into a shapeless, foul slime. "Our King truly fights for His people!" — Steven exclaimed. "With his stones, on his head," — Rock laughed. — "History repeats itself." With the warlord of "Yoke" removed, the four hunters entered the station's central command unhindered. There, they found no one. They penetrated the prince's throne room, but he was gone too. From the starship "Hunter," they were informed that a small ship had been detected minutes ago, leaving the station and heading into unknown space. "The station looks like a ruin from the outside," Jadon reported over the comms. "As far as I understand, the system inside has collapsed as well." "Yes, it's pretty deserted here in the command center," Captain Veren confirmed. "Now we must enter the City of the Doomed, where our enslaved brothers are. This is the final part of our mission — 'Restoration.'" The hunters entered the city. It was clear that a fierce battle had taken place here as well. Now, a ghostly silence lay between the tall buildings. The city streets were shrouded in smoke and ash. Among broken glass storefronts of skyscrapers, rolled piles of charcoal. On the central boulevard, the four hunters were met by Edreal and a huge crowd of men, women, and children. Two days later, the "Mercy" system dispatched passenger and trade ships for the inhabitants of the City of the Doomed. They left "Yoke" forever, heading to their new homeland, led by the starship "Hunter."

www.ingramcontent.com/pod-product-compliance
Lightning Source LLC
Chambersburg PA
CBHW071840190726
48292CB00005B/1854